WHAT A FUNNY THING TO SAY!

WHAT A FUNNY THING TO SAY!

by Bernice Kohn

pictures by R. O. Blechman

The Dial Press / New York

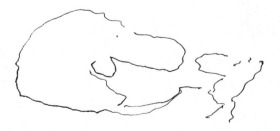

Text copyright © 1974 by Bernice Kohn
Pictures copyright © 1974 by The Dial Press
All rights reserved. No part of this book may be
reproduced in any form or by any means without the
prior written permission of the publisher, excepting
brief quotes used in connection with reviews written
specifically for inclusion in a magazine or newspaper.
Library of Congress Catalog Card Number: 73–6023
Printed in the United States of America/Third Printing, 1975
Design by Jane Byers Bierhorst

Library of Congress Cataloging in Publication Data

Hunt, Bernice Kohn.
What a funny thing to say!

Summary: Discusses briefly the origins of the English
language and the derivation of certain words, idioms,
and slang expressions.
Bibliography: p.
1. English language—Etymology—Juvenile literature.
2. English language—Slang—Juvenile literature.
[1. English language—Etymology] I. Blechman, R. O.,
illus. II. Title.
PE1574.H83   422   73-6023
ISBN 0-8037-9048-1
ISBN 0-8037-9079-1 (lib. bdg.)

For Morton, who taught me to play Stinky Pinky—
and many other things as well

CONTENTS

1
FROM SOUNDS
TO SONNETS

Long, long ago before there were such things as language or words as we know them now, people communicated with each other as best they could. There isn't anyone around to tell us exactly how they did it—but we can guess. When a caveman suddenly broke into a fast run he made it clear to any other cave people around that he heard, smelled, saw, or somehow sensed danger. Most likely they all ran too because he had communicated. And maybe as men grew more sophisticated, they learned to point. If the thing pointed to was a wolf or a bear, it is even possible that in time some caveman equivalent of *bowwow, woof-woof,* or *grr* was used to tell those who couldn't see what was coming around the bend.

In fact, scholars who have studied language and its origins actually use the term *bowwow theory* to mean that early man may have begun to speak by imitating animal sounds. It should be pointed out, however, that there are many other scholars who think this theory is ridiculous.

Another academic theory is called *pooh-pooh* or *yo-he-ho.* This one holds that the first repeated sounds were grunts of pain or exertion, or cries of surprise, anger, joy, and other emotions.

Actually, no one knows how language began and no one ever will since there are no written records to tell us about it. We do have reason to assume, however, that language was extremely simple at first and then changed and grew over a period of thousands of years. Initially, only genuinely basic needs, those necessary to survival, were expressed. But in time even primitive societies developed large vocabularies and highly complex systems of grammar and usage.

We follow the same pattern ourselves when we travel in a foreign land where the language is strange to us. Most of us learn to ask, "Where is the bathroom, please?" or "Where can I get something to eat?" on the day of arrival. It may be years before we learn the language well enough to describe a sunset or to write a poem. Initially, we make do with a few words that take care of our basic needs. Given enough time, we learn to express ideas that are completely abstract, such as those that deal with emotions. Once we have acquired a large enough vocabulary, we can learn to describe things in a precise and accurate way.

To give some idea of how enormously language has developed since the long-ago time of its murky beginnings, consider the following. If we decide, for the sake of discussion, to go along with the bowwow theory, we believe that when early man saw a dog he said, "Bowwow." Much, much later, when the idea of numbers began to dawn upon him, man said, "One bowwow," and, maybe, "Many bowwows" when he saw two or more dogs. It was a big step to be able to express the difference between *one* and *some*. It was an even bigger step to be able to say exactly how many dogs there were.

Now surely you have no trouble describing the number of animals you see. If the precise number is important, you say, "I see six dogs." When it is not of interest, you might say, "I see a pack of dogs." Or, as the case might be, "a swarm of wasps," or "a school of fish."

Pack, swarm, and *school* are all ways to describe a group of animals of one kind. There are many such terms in the English language—so many that only the most learned scholar is likely to know them all. Even the list that follows is far from complete.

A bevy of larks.
A cete of badgers.
A colony of ants.
A covert of coots.
A covey of partridges.
A drift of hogs.
A drove of sheep.
A flight of birds.
A flock of goats.
A gaggle of geese.
A gam of whales.
A gang of buffalo.

A herd of elephants.
A muster of peacocks.
A nide of pheasants.
A pod of seals.
A pride of lions.
A shrewdness of apes.
A skein of wild fowl.
A skulk of foxes.
A sloth of bears.
A sord of mallards.
A wisp of snipe.

If many of these words are new to you, don't be upset. You will be learning new words all your life—and you will never learn them all. Any individual's use of language depends on his background, his education, his curiosity, and his interest in language in general and words in particular.

Words are indispensable to our mode of living. They enable us to say exactly what we mean; to tell people what we think and feel and need; and to help us understand clearly the thoughts and feelings of others. It's true that at times we all use nonverbal language too. You can express yourself quite clearly with a look, a touch, or a simple action like slamming a door or hurling a plate. But if you have any question at all about how important spoken or written words are to your daily life, try getting along without them for just a few hours. You will soon see that words are our most important bridges to each other.

Words are necessary for more than day-to-day personal communication. Without words there would be no books; we would be a people without a history. Without words we could have no science, for science, by its very nature, can flourish only with the free exchange of precise information. In fact, if language had never developed, we would all be as primitive as cavemen.

How is it then that humans have developed words? Not words for one language alone but words for 2,796 languages—for that is the estimated number spoken today.

If we travel back to the distant past, we can discover a little about how some of those languages came into being. And while we are exploring languages, we will begin to understand how the approximately one-half million words in the English language evolved.

2
IT'S ALL
IN THE FAMILY

In the year 1786 Sir William Jones, a British chief justice in India, gave an address before a learned society in London. Sir William announced that he had studied Hindustani, and had concluded that Sanskrit (from which Hindustani is in part derived), Latin, and Greek had more similarities in their verb roots and forms of grammar than could possibly have been produced by accident. These similarities were so strong, Sir William thought, that no one learned in languages could examine all three without believing that they sprang from some common source—a source which perhaps no longer existed.

By 1786 *linguistics*, the study of language as a science, was already established. The elements of Greek and Latin in European languages had long been recognized and did not pose any great mystery. Both the Greeks and the Latin-speaking Romans had ruled large areas of Europe in ancient times, and it did not seem especially odd that some of their words and grammatical constructions remained behind their retreating armies.

But Sanskrit? Sanskrit was the literary language of India that had come into use about 1200 B.C. It had not been a living language for hundreds of years and existed only in Indian sacred writings. Everyone knew that there were words that sounded alike in Spanish and Italian or in German and Dutch, but how could there possibly be any connection between any of those languages and Sanskrit? Or between Sanskrit and English? A large-scale investigation was touched off, and the results of it, still accumulating, provide the basis for all of our knowledge of the subject.

The investigation had a unique feature, for it is normal procedure to learn history from written records. But of course in this case there were no early written records, and so it was done the other way around: First the languages were studied and then the history was pieced together.

The story, briefly, is this. Long ago, between about 2000 and 3000 B.C., a people called *Arya* in Sanskrit lived in Asia Minor. In English we refer to them as Indo-Europeans (although we still use the adjective *Aryan*). Most of the languages of Europe are descended from Indo-European, which proved to be Sir William's common source that no longer exists. We can tell this because many familiar words, *mother, father, brother,* names of numbers, and some plants and animals, are either almost identical in many languages, or close enough to be unquestionably related.

At some point in time, probably about 2000 B.C., the Indo-European people began to be crowded out of their homeland by certain tribes that swarmed in from Asia. The Indo-Europeans scattered in all directions and gradually made their way westward across Europe, and then to the British Isles, Scandinavia, and Crete. Finally they traveled to such distant places as Persia, Afghanistan, and India.

As groups of Indo-Europeans settled in various places, they were cut off from their former countrymen. Although they started out speaking only their own language, in time they began to learn the languages of the countries they were in as well. They also learned words from other migrants who arrived from faraway places. Little by little they mixed the languages and began to develop new words and pronunciations of their own. In this way, as the Indo-European civilizations grew over several thousands of years, they brought to Europe and Asia not one language but a vast family of languages.

Indo-European languages are used today by more than a billion people—almost a quarter of the world's population. These languages include English, German, and the Scandinavian tongues; French, Spanish, Italian, Portuguese and Romanian; Russian and other Slavic languages; Greek, Gaelic, and Welsh; Hindi, Urdu, Punjabi—and many other languages as well.

In spite of this impressive array there were many areas that the Indo-European adventurers either never reached, or where, for one reason or another, they failed to impose their own language, but adopted existing ones.

That means that there are many non-Indo-European languages in the world. These too fall into family groups based on strong similarities in the key words. The languages include Finnish, Hungarian, Turkish, Arabic, Hebrew, Chinese, Japanese, Malay, and a large group of African languages. (A complete list of the families and their major languages will be found in the Appendix at the end of this book.)

For every one of the many languages that exist, there are endless dialects and variations. It is hard to say where one draws the line and calls a dialect a separate language. An Italian-speaking Sicilian and an Italian-speaking Florentine may be completely unable to understand each other. So might a French-speaking Parisian and a French-speaking Haitian. For that matter a Yankee from Maine could well have some language difficulties in Georgia.

But for all the problems of noncomprehension within a particular language and within language families, there is no question whatsoever about the strength of family ties. Here are comparisons of just two words in a few of the Indo-European languages:

ENGLISH   *brother*
Sanskrit   bhrátá
Persian   birádar
Russian   brat
Latin   frater
Greek   phrater
German   Bruder
Irish   bhrathair

ENGLISH	*mother*
French	mère
Latin	mater
Spanish	madre
Portuguese	mãe
Italian	madre
Rumanian	mama
Swedish	moder
Danish	mor
Norwegian	mor
German	Mutter
Icelandic	módir
Dutch	moeder
Flemish	moeder
Russian	mat'
Czech	matko
Polish	matko
Bulgarian	maika

Such comparisons could go on and on, but just these two examples make it clear that language families do exist. And having established that, it's time to hurry through a little more history in order to catch up to the English we use every day.

3
HOW TO
MAKE A WORD

The English language we speak is, of course, made up of words. If you think really hard about words, you can get fairly silly. Did you ever wonder why a table is called a *table?* Why isn't it called a *sklush?* You might say that since English is an Indo-European language, *table* must be related to some word in that lost early tongue. But why didn't the Indo-Europeans call a table a *sklush?* Maybe they just didn't think of it. Or maybe the first person who said the Indo-European equivalent of *table* had some reason to feel that the object just looked like a table. We don't know and can't possibly find out. The earliest forms of our words and the circumstances surrounding their creation will have to remain shrouded in mystery. But once we reach the era of written language, the picture becomes clearer.

If you turn to the table of Indo-European languages on page 80 you will see that English falls into the Teutonic or German group. That is because English developed mainly from Anglo-Saxon, the language of the Angles, the Saxons, and the Jutes, Germanic tribes who settled in Britain during the fifth and sixth centuries A.D. Anglo-Saxon was very much like some German dialects. But about nine hundred years ago, life in Britain began to change.

To put it briefly, the Normans (Scandinavians who had settled in the province of Normandy in France only a century earlier) conquered England in 1066 and brought to that land their own languages, French and Latin. These became the official languages of England for the next three hundred years, although the common people continued to speak Anglo-Saxon. Then, during the fifteenth century, the Renaissance revival of learning and trade brought to British shores travelers who spoke Greek, Arabic, and Italian, which must have added considerably to the confusion. Later, when British colonists settled in the New World, they brought along their language, and English eventually became the language of the United States.

As a result of many political and cultural changes, the language we speak today is something of a mixed salad of other languages. Some of our words are derived from pure Anglo-Saxon, pure Latin, French, or whatever, while many other words are combinations of two or more languages joined together.

The blending took time, and long before we arrived at anything like modern English we passed through some earlier versions of it. Old English (Anglo-Saxon) was used from the eighth century (or possibly earlier—this date comes from the first written records) until the end of the eleventh century. Most of us probably wouldn't have understood a word of it. As an example, this is how the Lord's Prayer looked in Old English:

Faeder ure þu ðe eart on heofonum si þin nama
gehalgod. Tobecume þin rice. Gewurðe þin willa
on eorðan swa swa on hoefonum. Urne gedaeghwamlican
hlaf syle us to daeg. And forgyf us ure gyltas swa swa we
forgyfaþ urum gyltendem. And ne gelaed þu us on
costnunge ac alys us of yfele. Soð lice.

As Old English began to blend with Latin and French
it gradually changed into Middle English, which remained in use from the middle of the twelfth century
until the middle of the fifteenth century. By that time,
it had evolved into the earliest form of the modern English that we use today. Middle English clearly shows us
that Modern English was on its way. The following
stanza is from a poem by Geoffrey Chaucer, who lived
from about 1340 to 1400. Although some of the words
look a bit odd, it is easy to understand most of them.

Forth, pilgrim, forth! Forth, beste, out of they stal!
Know thy contree, look up, thank God of al;
Hold the hye wey, and lat thy gost thee lede:
And trouthe shall delivere, hit is no drede.

Even though these Middle English words are short and
fairly simple, we know that long before Chaucer's time

the language was already a mixture of many tongues. With the passage of years English grew more and more complex, so that by now, unraveling the construction of many of our words is a task for scholars.

The study of the history and development of words is called *etymology*. People who make a profession of etymology are called etymologists and they approach their subject in a serious and scientific way. The rest of us, though, can dip into words in a much more lighthearted fashion.

Even though this chapter is called "How to Make a Word," some of our words are not made at all, but are "born" ready-made into the language. Chief among these are the *onomatopoeic* words, words that imitate the sounds they describe, such as *buzz, clang, crash, splash, purr, fizz, sizzle, pop, snap, whir.*

Some other words came full-born into English from other languages. Throughout the Americas many of the place names are adopted from Indian languages. In the United States about half our states have Indian names, among them Oklahoma (*red people*), Mississippi (*big river*), and Michigan (*big lake*). We also have places called Ossining (*stony place*), Ticonderoga (*brawling water*), and Shenandoah (*daughter of the skies*).

Then there are the words that have come to us right from the Anglo-Saxon with only minor changes and no additions. They make up about 40 per cent of our English words, but since they are, by and large, our most frequently used words, they account for a much larger percentage of our daily vocabularies. Many of the Anglo-Saxon words are first-grade-reader words—*a, an, but, slow, fast, good, come, go, girl, and so forth* (yes, *and so forth*, too). They are all short, pithy words that don't really lend themselves to dissection or a great deal of analysis.

But what happens when we take a good etymological look at a more complicated word like *automobile? Auto* comes from *autos,* the Greek word for *self; mobile* is from *mobilis,* Latin for *movable.* So, broken down, the word means *self-movable.*

Auto- begins the word *automobile* and is called a *prefix.* Here are some other words that begin with the prefix *auto-.* Do you know what they all mean? If you don't, can you figure out their meanings?

autobiography
autograph
autohypnosis
autosuggestion

Knowing the meaning of a prefix can often provide the clue to understanding a new word. Here are some common Latin and Greek prefixes with their meanings and one example of how each is used. See if you can think of other words that begin with the same prefixes:

ante-	before	anteroom
anti-	against	antidote
cata-	down	catapult
de-	down	depressed
extra-	beyond, outside of	extrasensory
hyper-	over, above, in large amount	hypercritical
hypo-	under	hypodermic
in-	in, on, upon, within, into	inject
infra-	below	infrared
inter-	between, among	international
intra-	within	intramural
retro-	backward	retrospect
sub-	under	subway
trans-	across	transcontinental

In many of these examples the prefix is attached to a word *root,* one of the basic elements from which words can be formed. A good example of a word root is *graph,* which means *something written.* By attaching different prefixes to graph we can make *Addressograph, lithograph, phonograph, photograph, seismograph, telegraph, autograph,* and *stenography.* In *stenography,* the root came in the middle of a word. It can also come at the beginning as in *graphic,* and in this particular case it can even stand alone as *graph.*

Sometimes word roots are joined together to form words. *Monogamy* is formed from the root *monos* (*one*) and the Greek word *gamos* (*marriage*). Some other roots are:

anthropos	man
logos	knowledge, study, word
polys	many
theos	god

Consider, then, the words *anthropology, polygamy, monologue, theology*. Can you define them all? Can you think of other words based on the same roots?

The following is a list of Latin words which form the roots of many English words. See how many of the English words you can think of. Example: Latin—*ambulare*, to go about, to walk. English—*ambulatory, perambulator, ambulance, amble.*

aqua	water
cantus	song
fabula	story
forma	plan
frater	brother
labor	work
littera	letter
luna	moon
magnus	great
multus	much, many
navis	ship

pater	father
pugnus	fist
rota	wheel
unus	one

Even though off to a good start with prefixes and roots, it's useful to be able to finish what you start—and word endings are often most important. Endings that change the meanings of words are called *suffixes*. A common one is *-ist*, a person who does something, as a *dramatist*, a *machinist*, or a *violinist*. Here is a list of suffixes and one example of a word that ends with each. See if you can think of enough other words to guess the meaning of the suffix:

-ade	lemonade
-ant	deodorant
-dom	kingdom
-ent	reverent
-ese	Japanese
-ess	lioness
-est	largest
-ful	cheerful
-hood	childhood
-ing	galloping
-ion	convention
-ite	Wisconsinite
-less	careless

-ment	enjoyment
-ness	happiness
-ster	prankster
-ward	downward

Words constructed of roots, prefixes, and suffixes are fairly common in English, and with a little practice their origins are easily figured out. There is another class of words, however, with origins you could never figure out. These are based not on word elements but on individual, and often amusing, histories. For example, did you ever hear of an *antimacassar?* It was a kind of lace doily once very much in fashion, used on the back and arms of a chair to protect the upholstery. You undoubtedly had forebears who used them and called them by name, but probably few realized what the name meant. It actually came from a gooey hair oil that was popular in its day and apparently oiled upholstery as well as hair. This word used the prefix *anti-,* meaning *against*—and the brand name of the hair oil, *Macassar.*

The sandwich, which is familiar to all of us, is named for John Montagu, 4th Earl of Sandwich, a Briton who died in 1792. It is said that the Earl was so addicted to gambling that he couldn't tear himself away from the card table long enough to eat a proper meal. When he was hungry, he ordered his servants to place his dinner between two slices of bread and bring it to him while he played.

The fish that we know as halibut today belongs to a class of fishes which were all called *butte* in Old English. The very largest *buttes* were saved for religious holy days, and since *holy* was spelled *haly*, the large *buttes* were called *haly buttes*.

A lady named Amelia Jenks Bloomer was strangely honored by having a silly-looking article of clothing named after her. Back in 1851 it was the custom for ladies to wear long skirts with layers of billowing petticoats underneath, but then as now there were women who defied custom in the interest of progress. One of them was daring enough to appear in public in a short skirt, but she took care to protect her modesty by wearing long, full trousers underneath which were gathered around her ankles. This amazing costume was written about by Mrs. Bloomer, who owned a small newspaper called *The Lily*. She apparently captured the public's imagination by her description of what she delicately referred to as "sanitary attire." Lacking any better name, her readers soon began to call the funny pants *bloomers*.

Mrs. Bloomer was not the only one to be immortalized by pants. There was an eighteenth-century landowner in New York State named Harmen Knickerbocker who was well known in his neighborhood because he was an extremely wealthy man. In the early 1800s Washington Irving wrote a book that gently made fun of the Dutch farmers of the area, and as a joke signed the book with the false name, "Knickerbocker." The book became known as "Knickerbocker's History of New York," and since it contained many pictures of early Dutch settlers in their knee breeches, these pants acquired the name *knickerbockers*—later shortened to *knickers*.

Before we leave the subject of pants, we should examine the word *diaper*. This was originally the name of a fine white cloth that was used for church robes and later for table linen. But as time passed, the word *diaper* ceased to mean either of these things. Today we know it simply as the piece of soft white cloth that is pinned around a baby.

In 1713 Captain Andrew Robinson of Gloucester, Massachusetts, launched a new type of ship which he had designed and built. As the graceful craft slid gently into the water an impressed bystander murmured, "Oh, how she *scoons!*" Captain Robinson liked the sound of the strange word so much that he decided to call his vessel a *scooner*. Sometime later, the word picked up an *h* and became *schooner*.

Many words owe their existence to error. One such word is *assassin*. During the crusades in the eleventh century, a group of fanatical Persians formed a religious sect which practiced terrorist killings of Christians. Since the terrorists frequently smoked hashish before their missions, they were called in Arabic, *hashshāshīn, hash-ish-eaters*. Europeans hearing the word not only mispronounced it but understood it to mean *one who murders*.

Many, many words spring from poor pronunciation. *Patter* is an example that dates from the Middle Ages when few people were literate. Churchgoers dutifully recited their prayers in Latin without understanding a word of what they were saying. *Pater Noster*, "Our Father" in Latin, was usually pronounced "patternoster," and *patter* remains our word for a swift, meaningless stream of chatter.

Bedlam comes to us from a fifteenth-century mental hospital in London, the hospital of St. Mary of Bethlehem. In those days the general atmosphere of a mental hospital was indeed bedlam. *Bethlehem* was contracted to *bedlam* by the London Cockneys, and the word has remained with us today to mean any kind of noisy confusion.

Another word that is the result of a Cockney contraction is *tawdry*. Cheap and gaudy lace neckerchiefs called St. Audrey's lace used to be sold at church fairs. As the hawkers shouted, "St. Audrey's lace!" it sounded like "tawdry lace." And finally it was shortened to just *tawdry*.

Not all word histories date from long ago. The Frisbee, a popular plastic disc toy, was invented—and named—by a building inspector in Los Angeles. When he sent one of his creations soaring through the air it reminded him (for reasons which remain mysterious) of the pie tins used by the Frisbie Bakery in Bridgeport, Connecticut.

4
LANGUAGE IS
ALIVE AND WELL

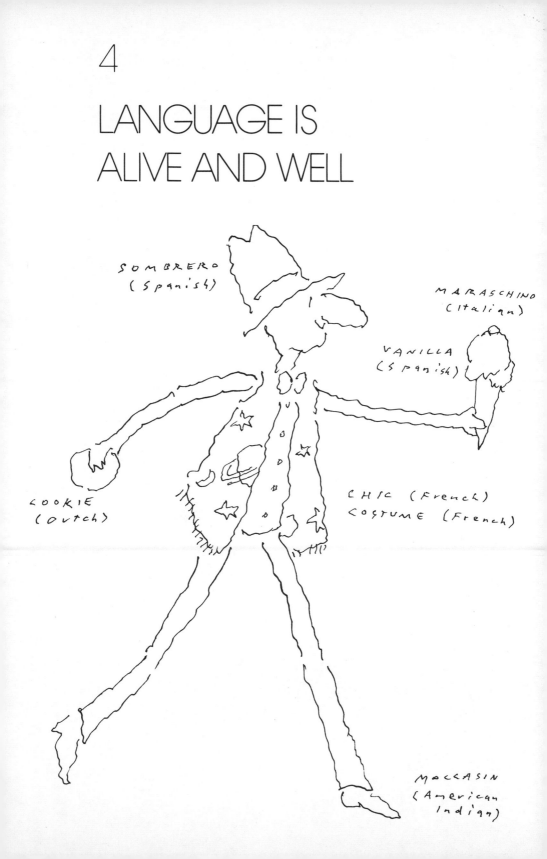

SOMBRERO
(Spanish)

MARASCHINO
(Italian)

VANILLA
(Spanish)

COOKIE
(Dutch)

CHIC (French)
COSTUME (French)

MOCCASIN
(American
Indian)

In the last chapter we explored words made of "spare parts," and some words derived from names, misunderstandings, and poor pronunciations. Many of these words have been part of the English language for a long time.

But English, like any other living language, never stops changing and growing. It must always keep up with the technology and culture of the people who use it. Sometimes the change is practically automatic; it simply grows out of natural events.

In modern times travel grew commonplace, and people began to journey to different countries, often bringing back a smattering of foreign words. If the words filled a need in English, they remained to become a permanent part of the language. Foreign words also entered our language with the great waves of immigration that brought people from many lands to American shores during the nineteenth and twentieth centuries. It was only natural that many words from their different languages seeped into our own and enriched it.

If you think you don't speak any language but English you might be surprised to know how many foreign words you have in your vocabulary. You probably know most of the words which follow. They can all be found in an English dictionary.

FRENCH

à la carte	foyer
bagatelle	garage
ballet	hors d'oeuvre
boulevard	menu
chapeau	nonchalance
chauffeur	personnel
chic	promenade
costume	rendezvous
cuisine	repertoire
discothèque	sabotage

SPANISH

adobe	corral	patio
armada	desperado	plaza
arroyo	fiesta	rodeo
bonanza	guerilla	siesta
bronco	gusto	sombrero
burro	lasso	tornado
canyon	mosquito	vanilla
cargo		

ITALIAN

bravo	presto
cameo	prima donna
macaroni	regatta
maraschino	soprano
piano	studio
piccolo	tarantula

ARABIC
(These words have some changes due to differences in the alphabets)

alcohol	sultan
algebra	talisman
mattress	tariff
sheik	zero

YIDDISH

chutzpa	nebbish
kibitz	shlemiel
kosher	shmaltz
mensh	

And for good measure add a few odds and ends like *tea* (Chinese), *moccasin* (American Indian), *orangutan* (Malayan), *trek* (Afrikaans), *kindergarten* (German), *bungalow* (Hindi), *cookie* (Dutch). You can probably think of many more.

While the adoption of foreign words is one way to keep a language up to date, it isn't the only way. Advances in technological and scientific fields always call for new words. The need is sometimes met by the use of roots, prefixes, and suffixes, and often by pure invention.

Obviously the age of scientific discovery has given English innumerable new words, such as *airplane, locomotive, tractor, electricity, submarine, helicopter, hydrofoil, stereophonic, air conditioner, refrigerator,* and *astronaut.* For every new development a new word.

In general, scientific words show less variety in their origins than everyday words. Many scientific words come only from Greek elements—*psychology, psychiatry, chlorophyll, podiatry, phobia, mania.* Medical vocabulary is predominantly Latin, including the names of the parts of the body and the pharmaceuticals. Scientists use Latin names for plants and animals too. This is important because it makes these terms identical in all parts of the world. Because Arabs were the first great mathematicians, many of our mathematical and astronomical terms come from the Arabic—*zenith, nadir, cipher, algebra.*

Some words have been adopted from the names of inventors or discoverers—*watt* (James Watt), *diesel* (Rudolph Diesel), *ampere* (André Marie Ampère), *pasteurize* (Louis Pasteur), *farad* (Michael Faraday), *Ferris wheel* (G. W. G. Ferris), *volt* (Count Alessandro Volta). Other words are compressions of two or more words—*turboprop, turboramjet;* many nearly unpronounceable scientific names are reduced merely to initials—*DNA* (deoxyribonucleic acid), *DDT* (dichlorodiphenyltrichloroethane), *TNT* (trinitrotoluene).

Among the more amusing new words are those abbreviations called *acronyms,* words formed from initials, or initials plus parts of words:

CORE   *Congress of Racial Equality*
jeep   *General Purpose*

laser	*Light Amplification by Stimulated Emission of Radiation*
maser	*Microwave Amplification by Stimulated Emission of Radiation*
NATO	*North Atlantic Treaty Organization*
radar	*Radio Detecting and Ranging*
scuba	*Self-Contained Underwater Breathing Apparatus*
snafu	*Situation Normal All Fouled Up*
sonar	*Sound detecting and Ranging*
WAAC	*Women's Army Auxiliary Corps*
WAVES	*Women Accepted for Voluntary Emergency Service*
WHO	*World Health Organization*
zip (code)	*Zone Improvement Plan*

5
LANGUAGE IS ALIVE
–AND COLORFUL

We have seen how our language grows with the addition of foreign and technological words. Once such words have firmly entered the vocabulary, they become respectable and can then make their way into the dictionary. Although some of them may fall into disuse and become obsolete, the great majority are here to stay.

But there is another class of new words that enters the language through the back door. These words may or may not ever gain either respectability or permanence. They can be lumped together loosely under the headings of *colloquialisms* and *slang*. The dividing line between the two is often unclear.

Colloquial words or expressions are actually in good repute, but are considered informal. *Hi, O.K., so long,* and *stuck-up* are all in the dictionary but marked *informal* or *colloq*. That means that they are perfectly acceptable in everyday speech between friends but would be highly improper in formal speech, serious writing, or conversation with a dignitary.

Slang is a bit further down the ladder of good form. Even though we all use it, it is not correct. It may or may not appear in the dictionary, but if it does, it is clearly labeled *slang*. Slang is often highly colorful language. It includes words that are used by almost everybody as well as words that are used only by a smaller subculture such as an age or ethnic group.

Slang comes and goes with changing fads and fashions. Although some slang words do make their way into the respectable vocabulary, they are generally considered impermanent. The last few generations have witnessed the arrival and passing of *twenty-three skidoo*, *zoot suit*, *Ish Kabibble*, *bobby-soxer*, *cat's pajamas*, and *groovy*.

Slang that is used by the public at large is often short-cut language. When you mention that a man was *bumped off*, you develop a bit of colorful imagery with few words. The mere term *bumped off* conjures up a feeling of gangsterism and of murder rather than accidental death. It would require several proper sentences to create the same picture that *bumped off* does in two words.

Common slang often substitutes an acceptable word for a "bad" word. Anyone can say, "Darn it," or "Gee whiz," without risk of offending even the most prim listener.

Subculture slang, however, serves different purposes. In addition to being used in the ordinary way, slang may describe objects or situations for which there are no suitable all-purpose words; it may be used as a password to identify members of the group to each other; and it may be used as a secret language that is incomprehensible to any outsiders listening in. The last usage is an important factor in both the impermanence and creation of much slang. When the public *catches on* (*colloq.*) to a private subculture word and begins to use it, the subculture immediately adopts a new word, which remains *in* (*slang*) until it too becomes known to the public.

Related to subculture slang and frequently overlapping it is *jargon,* the special language of a profession or industry. Jargon is usually not intended to be a secret language; its chief purpose is accurate and/or brief communication among those within a profession. In practice, however, jargon is often just as incomprehensible to the outsider as any deliberately private vocabulary. Sometime try to understand what your doctor says to his nurse.

Computer experts speak of *programs, bits, hardware,* and *software.* These are everyday words, but in computer jargon they all have different meanings. A *program* is information that is coded for use in a computer; a *bit* (from *BI*nary digi*T*) is a unit of information based on a computer language of two digits such as 0 and 1; *hardware* is the actual computer machinery; *software* refers to the set of programs and procedures that are used in the operation of a computer. You can see why jargon is a useful short cut for the computer ingroup.

People in advertising, show business, the space program, pop music, and the armed forces have their own jargon; so do hobbyists of all kinds, sportsmen, railroad workers, students, drug users, truck drivers, doctors, social workers, members of the underworld, and so forth.

The hippie subculture of the 1960s enriched the language (at least temporarily) with a variety of terms which spread into the popular vocabulary almost overnight. Among them:

crash pad	a place to spend the night.
drop out (verb)	to withdraw from anything distasteful—society, school, work, etc.
flower child	one who tries to live in a natural way rejecting all material or commercial values.
flower power	the attempt to change society through peace and love.
freak (noun)	one who likes or believes in a certain thing, such as rock freak, food freak.
freak (verb) or freak out	to have an extreme drug experience; to lose touch with reality; to shock others by bizarre appearance or behavior.
groovy	great, marvelous, happy, joyous.
hairy or heavy	frightening, worrisome, bad. *Heavy* can also mean sincere, meaningful, profound.
hung up	unable to make a decision *or* inhibited.
up tight	tense, anxious, rigid.

Sometimes slang words are simply shortened words—*psycho* for psychotic, *mike* for microphone. Often they are repetitions—*flip-flop, flim-flam, okey-dokey, itsy-bitsy*.

Moving on to a higher order of creation are the rhyming terms. Some of these are so common that they need no definition—*sure cure, hot shot, nitwit, hot rod, eager beaver*. Others are less common and some of them marvelously imaginative:

beat feet	to hurry
brag rags	military decorations
chopper-copper	a greedy eater
culture vulture	person interested in the arts
date bait	a pretty girl
face lace	whiskers
fem sem (also hen pen)	a girls' school
finger wringer	a very emotional actor
freak beak	a large nose
handsome ransom	a large sum of money
hick dick	a small town policeman
jug mug	a convict
loud shroud	colorful clothing
lush mush	good food
ptomaine domain	a bad restaurant
sudsy dudsy	laundromat

While these American terms have an undeniable charm, rhyming slang reached the proportions of an art form among the thieves of early- to mid-nineteenth-century

London. This was an outstanding case of a "slanguage" that existed for the twin purposes of identifying members of the subculture to each other and keeping secrets from outsiders who might overhear a conversation. Although rhyming slang spread to Australia with the British convicts who settled there (they were exiled instead of imprisoned), it is still generally known as Cockney Rhyming Slang.

The principle of the language is simple—a slang phrase that means something different from the real word but rhymes with it is used in its place. Speaking the language is far from simple to anyone who is not thoroughly familiar with it. Here is a small vocabulary so that you can try your skill.

COCKNEY RHYMING SLANG

SLANG TERM	REAL MEANING
apples and pears	stairs
babbling brook	crook
bees and honey	money
birch broom	room
Bopeep	sleep; asleep
bottle and stopper	copper (policeman)
bowl of chalk	talk
bug and flea	tea
butter and beers	ears
Cain and Abel	table
cheese and kisses	the Mrs.

cough and sneeze	cheese
daisy roots	boots
dickory dock	sock
Dickey dirt	shirt
fiddle and flute	suit
fields of wheat	street
fisherman's daughter	water
flowery dell	prison cell
flying kite	night
give and take	cake
happy half hours	flowers
heart of oak	broke
husband and wife	knife
Isabella	umbrella
I suppose	nose
Joe Blake	steak
John Hop	cop
jug and pail	jail
lean and fat	hat
Lilley and Skinner	dinner
linen draper	newspaper
loaf of bread	head
Pat and Mick	sick
plates of meat	feet
skin and blister	sister
struggle and strife	wife
sugar and honey	money
whistle and flute	suit

A VERY SHORT STORY

I went up the apples and pears to find my struggle and strife Bopeep. I figured she was Pat and Mick, so I made her some bug and flea. Later she asked for fisherman's daughter and a linen draper, so I put on my dickory docks and fiddle and flute. Before I left the birch broom I put some bees and honey in my dickey dirt, took my Isabella, and made for the fields of wheat. I got a Joe Blake for Lilley and Skinner and some happy half hours for cheese and kisses and made it back before flying kite.

6
A CLUTCH
OF CLICHÉS

Clichés are funny. Most of the time we don't realize how funny they are. That's because of the very nature of a cliché—it is a trite or overused expression or idea. It is just because clichés are so overused that we don't pay much attention to them. The first time someone said he was a "bundle of nerves," it must have sounded very clever and original. After many admiring hearers copied the phrase, though, it became a cliché and people stopped noticing it.

One way to appreciate the humor in the following clichés is to draw a picture, either on paper or in your head, that shows exactly what the words say.

Alive and kicking.
Bored to tears.
Born with a silver spoon in one's mouth.

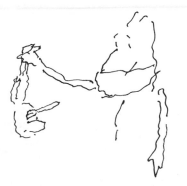

Cook one's goose.
Cost a pretty penny.
Done to a turn.
Eat one's heart out.

Face the music.
Fall head over heels in love.
A fish out of water.
Go to the dogs.

Have a green thumb.
A horse of another color.
In a nutshell.
In hot water.
Keep a stiff upper lip.
Kill two birds with one stone.

Leave no stone unturned.
Lend an ear.

Let the cat out of the bag.
On pins and needles.
Put the cart before the horse.
Read between the lines.
See eye to eye.
Stew in your own juice.
Through thick and thin.
Time flies.
Walking encyclopedia.

7
PIDGIN
ENGLISH

Once upon a time, some three hundred years ago, a few British merchants tried to ply their trade on the coast of China. They had a rather serious problem because they spoke no Chinese and the Chinese spoke no English. As a matter of fact, the businessmen didn't speak English any too well either. They were a fairly rough lot of adventurers with little schooling or interest in the fine points of their mother tongue. They were concerned with making money, and the quickest way to do it was to find some way to communicate with the Chinese in order to buy and sell.

The Britons thought the Chinese simple and childlike because they weren't "civilized" and able to speak the King's language; and since children usually learn baby talk before they learn to speak properly, it seemed that the thing to do was to communicate with the Chinese in baby talk.

The pupils turned out to be highly intelligent and they learned quickly. They did have trouble, however, with some English sounds that do not occur in Chinese, so they Chineseified some words and said *Melican* for American, *plopa* for proper, and so forth.

And the teachers, being neither able nor willing to take the time to teach grammar, simply tacked the

Chinese sound *ee* onto all verbs as an all-purpose ending.

Strange as the new language sounded, it worked, and within a short time business was being conducted in what the Englishmen named Business English. *Business,* however, was one of the words the Chinese found hard to say, and so it became Pidgin English instead.

Some time later, in 1788, the first English convicts settled in Australia and took with them not only their Cockney Rhyming Slang but some Pidgin English as well. The language proved effective in establishing relations with the Australian Aborigines, and it soon spread throughout the Pacific. Only the Maoris of New Zealand refused to have anything to do with Pidgin and so learned to speak excellent English instead.

Pacific Pidgin differs somewhat from Chinese Pidgin. The phrasing is not the same and the usual Pacific verb ending is *-em, -im,* or *-um,* all contractions of *him.* There is also a frequent use of *fella* which means *fellow, one, man,* or *boy.*

Today, Pidgin English is spoken by millions of people throughout the Orient, Australia, the islands of the Pacific, and in India, Malaya, and Africa. No matter what the locale, the language usually consists of about 300 to 400 English nouns, about 100 adjectives, and 50 verbs. It also uses a few native words.

Because Pidgin is spelled just the way it sounds, it is often hard to read. But pronounced aloud and actually heard, it is not hard to understand.

During World War II the U.S. Army issued a handbook of Pidgin English for American soldiers on duty in the South Pacific. It included a number of choice sentences for use in emergency situations. For example, a soldier who wanted to cry out, "Don't move or I'll shoot!" was advised to say, "Yufela yu stand fast. Yu no can walkabout. Suppose yufela walkabout me killim yu long musket."

Since you can't tell when it might be useful to have some Pidgin in your bag of tricks, here is a short vocabulary list:

ENGLISH	SOUTH PACIFIC PIDGIN ENGLISH
beard	grass bilong face
Do you understand?	Yu savvy?
fight *or* hit	faitim (*fight him*)
he *or* she	im
I don't understand.	Mi no har (*hear*) im gud. *or* Mi no har im savvy.
I want	mi like
It's far away.	Fella ee (*or* i) go go go go.
mine	bilong me
No.	no got
pocket	basket bilong trouser
small	liklik
Speak more slowly.	Yu no can tok (*talk*) hariap (*hurry up*).

the sun	lamp bilong Jesus
we	me fella *or* yu-me (if we includes person addressed)
What do you call it in Pidgin?	Dis fella samting (*something*) ere bilong wuh name?
What is your name?	Callim name bilong yu?
Where is the bathroom?	House peck peck, i stop where?
Where is the hotel?	House drink, i stop where?
Yes.	i got
yours	bilong yu

Now that you are an expert, here are some samples of Pidgin to practice with. The first is from Charles G. Leland's *Pidgin-English Sing-Song* and is in Chinese rather than South Pacific Pidgin.

Chinaman he makee allo-tim so-fashee China-side. Supposey on piecee fata flog he bull-chilo, supposey that chilo too muchee largo man, all-same olo man-he must catchee floggum, no other ting can do, wat-tim fata ni-ki he. Can makee cly-cly, no more can do. All-same fashion, putlutta floggee yangshee lutta, yeungki floggee nippa, haszeman floggee waifo, mata floggee kaichilos, massa floggee kungpatto, kungpatto floggee shaman.

TRANSLATION

A Chinaman always acts in this way in China. Suppose a father wants to flog his son; if that child is as big as a grown man, the father must catch him to flog him. He can make him cry but nothing more. In the same way an elder brother beats a younger brother, an uncle beats a nephew, a husband beats his wife, a mother beats her daughter, a master beats his steward, and a steward beats a servant.

The Christian missionaries who worked in the Pacific Islands probably found the following indispensable:

THE LORD'S PRAYER

Papa bilong mifela, yu stap long heven. Ol i-santuim nem nem bilong yu. Kingom bilong yu i-kam. Ol i-harim tok bilong yu long graun alsem long heven. Tude givim kaiaik bilong de long mifela. Forgivim rong bilong mifela, olsem mifela forgivim rong ol i-mekim long mifela. Yu no bringim mifela long traiim. Tekewe samting nogud long mifela.

PSALM XXIII 1–3

Big Name Watchum sheepsheep. Watchum black-fella. No more belly cry fella hab. Big Name makum camp alonga fraa, takum blackfella walkabout longa, no fightee, no more hurry wata. Big Boss longa sky makum inside glad; takem walkabout longa too much gudfella.

As a final offering in South Pacific Pidgin, here is a secular selection from a Pidgin magazine called *Frend Belong Mi*, published in New Guinea. Since the spellings are a bit obscure, some of them are explained below.

Wairless i gudfelol samting. Em i samting bilong hariap tru. Wanfelol master i sindaun long haf long liklik mashin, finger bilong em i faitim mashin, nau electik bilong mashin i salim tok i go longwe mor. Olrait, longwe mor wanfelol aderfelol master i sindaun long liklik mashin, em i save hirim disfelol tok.

i	he
gudfelol	goodfellow
samting	something
hariap tru	hurry up through
sindaun	sit down
mashin	machine
salim	sails
tok	talk
longwe	long way
olrait	all right
aderfelol	other fellow
save	savvy (understand)
hirim	hear

TRANSLATION

Wireless is good. It is swift. A man sits down at a small machine and taps with his finger, and electricity sends his message a long way. A long way away another man sits at another machine and understands the message.

8
FUN AND GAMES
WITH WORDS

Both Chinese and South Pacific Pidgin are distortions of English which owe their beginnings to trade—a serious enough purpose. But there are other distortions of English whose only purpose is fun. These are the secret languages that children everywhere have always spoken—to the puzzlement of their parents and teachers.

Most of the popular secret languages are based on the same principles: either the insertion of an extra syllable where it doesn't belong or the transposition of a part of a word to a different location.

Pig Latin, probably the most well known of all such languages, follows both of these principles. To form a word in Pig Latin you move the first letter (or the first two letters if they form a diphthong—two letters pronounced as one sound—such as *th-*, *st-*, *pr-*, etc.) to the end of the word and add the syllable *ay* to it. *Cat* becomes *atcay*. The sentences, *Can you read this? It is written in Pig Latin.* become: *Ancay ouyay eadray isthay? Itay isay ittenwray inay Igpay Atinlay.*

Similar but much simpler are languages known as Na, Gree, and Skimono Jive. They are all popular because they are so easy. For Na or Gree, add *-na* or *-gree* to the end of every word. The first line of "Mary Had a Little Lamb" becomes:

Maryna hadna ana littlena lambna, itsna fleecena wasna whitena asna snowna.

or

Marygree hadgree agree littlegree lambgree, itsgree fleecegree wasgree whitegree asgree snowgree.

To speak Skimono Jive, you add *sk-* to the beginning of every word:

Skmary skhad ska sklittle sklamb skits skfleece skwas skwhite skas sksnow.

All three of those languages are easy to speak, but not nearly so easy to understand, especially if they are being spoken rapidly, and the listeners don't know the system.

Ong is a somewhat harder language. It is formed by

adding the syllable *ong* before every vowel unless the vowel has no sound of its own, as the *e* at the end of *little* or *fleece*. You now get:

Mongary hongad onga longittle longamb, ongits flongeece wongas whongite ongas snongow.

Pelf Latin, or Alfalfa as it is called in some places, is even more difficult. The system with this one is to insert *lf* after every vowel or diphthong and then repeat that same vowel or diphthong:

Malfary halfad alfa lilfittle lalfamb, ilfits fleelfleece walfas whilfite alfas snolfow.

One of the hardest of all the secret languages is Tutnee. To form Tutnee the letter *u* is inserted after every consonant (or consonant diphthong) and then the consonant or diphthong is repeated so that every *t* becomes *tut*, every *r* becomes *rur*, and so forth. It works out like this:

Mumarury huhadud a lulituttutlule lulamumbub, itutsus fufluleecuce wuwasus whuwhitute asus snusnowuw.

There are any number of similar languages and they differ in various localities. Using the methods outlined here, perhaps you can make up a new one of your own.

There is only one fitting way to end this book and that is with the very best of all word games, Stinky Pinky. It is played by giving a definition for which the other player has to supply a pair of rhyming words of two syllables each (you can get ideas from the rhyming terms, page 47), such as *stinky pinky*. For example—Definition: A solid piece of furniture. Answer: A stable table. To make up questions, you have to think of the rhyming pair first, and then think up the definition.

The rhyming words do not have to be limited to two syllables. You can show how many syllables are called for by altering the words *stinky pinky* to the proper number of syllables: Stink Pink (1 syllable each), Stinkity Pinkity (3 syllables each) or Stinktinkity Pinktinkity (4 syllables each).

Are you ready? If your mind boggles, the answers are on pages 77–78.

A STINKY PINKY FOR:

1 / A mature fortune teller.
2 / A small spirit who does one's bidding.

3 / A one-of-a-kind old object.
4 / A dessert that's all upset.
5 / Something that is dark red and soars.
6 / A grumpy New Englander.
7 / A reptile with many offspring.
8 / A strong little flying animal.
9 / A beetle from the Middle East.
10 / A rabbit's cash.
11 / A not-so-happy man who fixes pipes.
12 / Two trapeze artists.

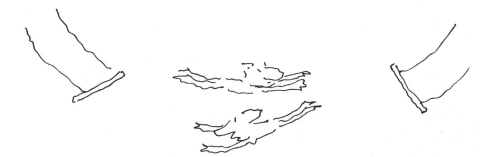

13 / A creature with eight legs that isn't as slim as it used to be.

A STINK PINK FOR:
1 / A double-jointed water fowl.
2 / Something to order in a seafood restaurant.
3 / A tent in a rainstorm.
4 / An animal that makes some people jump on chairs.
5 / What some animals leave on the barbershop floor.

A STINKITY PINKY FOR:

1 / A white-haired, pink-eyed large animal.
2 / An accurate fish.
3 / An incautious elf.

A STINKY PINKITY FOR:

1 / A nontransparent reptile.
2 / A famous communications instrument.
3 / A delicious summertime drink.

A STINKITY PINKITY FOR:

1 / A bottomless pit.
2 / A morose prickly animal.
3 / An authentic murder.
4 / A road with no advertising signs.
5 / A flea with poor manners.

A STINKTINKITY PINKTINKITY FOR:

1 / A happy funeral.

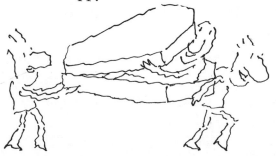

2 / A place to hatch reptiles.

3 / A law governing air travel.

4 / A teachers' strike.

ANSWERS TO STINKY PINKY

STINKY PINKY

1 / Adult occult.

2 / Teeny genie.

3 / Unique antique.

4 / Flustered custard.

5 / Maroon balloon.

6 / Cranky Yankee.

7 / Fertile turtle.

8 / Sturdy birdie.

9 / Arab scarab.

10 / Bunny money.

11 / Glummer plumber.

12 / Supple couple.

13 / Wider spider.

STINK PINK

1 / Loose goose.

2 / Fish dish.

3 / Damp camp.

4 / House mouse.

5 / Bear hair.

STINKITY PINKY

1 / Albino rhino.

2 / Unerring herring.

3 / Unwary fairy.

STINKY PINKITY

1 / Opaque rattlesnake.

2 / Well-known telephone.

3 / Homemade lemonade.

STINKITY PINKITY

1 / Day-and-night appetite.

2 / Saturnine porcupine.

3 / Bona fide homicide.

4 / Beautified countryside.

5 / Impolite parasite.

STINKTINKITY PINKTINKITY

1 / Merrymaking undertaking.

2 / Alligator incubator.

3 / Aviation legislation.

4 / Education demonstration.

We all use words every day in order to transmit and to receive information. Basically, of course, that is what words are for, but they offer many other possibilities if only we are alert to them. Words can bring us fascinating bits of history. It is challenging to explore their origins and constructions and to make words from the elements we know. Words are often funny. And best of all, words are fun. For those who take advantage of everything that words can offer, life may never be the same again!

APPENDIX

PARTIAL TABLE OF LANGUAGE FAMILIES

(Many minor languages have been omitted.)

INDO-EUROPEAN LANGUAGES

Teutonic
> English
>
> German
>
> Dutch
>
> Norwegian
>
> Swedish
>
> Danish
>
> Icelandic

Romance (deriving most from Roman Latin)
> French
>
> Spanish
>
> Italian
>
> Portuguese
>
> Romanian

Slavic
> Russian
>
> Polish
>
> Czech
>
> Slovakian
>
> Bulgarian
>
> Serbo-Croatian

Slovene

Baltic

Lithuanian

Lettish

Greek

Albanian

Armenian

Persian

Celtic

Gaelic

Erse (Scots Gaelic)

Welsh

Breton

Indic

Hindustani (Hindi and Urdu)

Bengali

Marathi

Punjabi

Rajasthani

URAL-ALTAIC LANGUAGES

The Finno-Ugric group

Lapp

Finnish

Estonian

Hungarian (Magyar)

Ostyak

Samoyed

The Turco-Tartar group
  Turkish
  Tartar
  Kirghiz

SEMITIC-HAMITIC LANGUAGES

Arabic
Hebrew
Ethiopian
Maltese
Cushite
Berber languages

SINO-TIBETAN LANGUAGES

Chinese
Tibetan
Siamese
Burmese

JAPANESE-KOREAN LANGUAGES
Japanese
Korean

MALAYO-POLYNESIAN LANGUAGES

Malay
Fiji
Tahitian

Maori
Hawaiian

DRAVIDIAN LANGUAGES

Tamil
Telugu
Malayalam

AFRICAN LANGUAGES

Hausa
Swahili
Kikuyu
Rwanda
Fula
Yoruba
Luba
Mandingo
Ibo
Somali
Zulu
Galla
Fanti

Other families include American Indian languages, Caucasian, Aboriginal Australian, Basque. Some languages remain unclassified.

BIBLIOGRAPHY

Adams, J. Donald, *The Magic and Mystery of Words*. New York, Holt, 1963.

Ayers, Donald M., *English Words from Latin and Greek Elements*. Tucson, The University of Arizona Press, 1965.

Barnett, Lincoln, *The Treasure of Our Tongue*. New York, Alfred A. Knopf, 1964.

Brook, G. L., *A History of the English Language*. New York, W. W. Norton and Co., 1964 (paper ed.).

Burgess, Anthony, *Language Made Plain*. New York, Thomas Y. Crowell, 1969 (paper ed.).

Funk, Charles Earle, *Thereby Hangs a Tale*. New York, Harper, 1950.

Funk, Wilfred, *Word Origins*. New York, Grosset and Dunlap, 1950.

Funk, Wilfred, and Lewis, Norman, *30 Days to a More Powerful Vocabulary*. New York, Pocket Books, 1971 (Revised paper ed.).

Nurmberg, Maxwell, and Rosenblum, Morris, *All About Words: An Adult Approach to Vocabulary Building*. Englewood Cliffs, Prentice-Hall, 1966.

Partridge, Eric, *A Dictionary of Clichés*. New York, E. P. Dutton, 1963 (paper ed.).

Pei, Mario, *The Story of Language*. New York, New American Library, 1960 (paper ed.).

INDEX

ABOUT THE AUTHOR

Bernice Kohn is the author of more than three dozen books for children and young adults, including SECRET CODES AND CIPHERS, THE BEACHCOMBERS' BOOK and THE ORGANIC LIVING BOOK. "Like all writers," she says, "I am fascinated by words." She is married to a well-known author of adult books, Morton Hunt. They live in East Hampton, New York, where they enjoy sailing, digging clams, and growing all their own vegetables in a completely organic garden.

ABOUT THE ARTIST

R. O. Blechman is the author-illustrator of several adult books, including TUTTO ESAURITO, ONION SOUP, NO, and THE JUGGLER OF OUR LADY. His animated films have been exhibited in London and New York City film festivals, and he is currently working on a half-hour TV film dealing with problems of overpopulation and malnutrition. Mr. Blechman lives with his wife, Moisha Kubinyi, and two children in New York City.